STO

ALLEN COUNTY PUBLIC LIBRARY

FRIENDS
OF ACPL

W9-CLD-418

Allen County Public Library

For my most precious gifts,
Stefani, Asa, Harley, Chloe
BB

First U.S. edition published in 2002
by Barron's Educational Series, Inc.
250 Wireless Blvd, Hauppauge, NY 11788
www.barronseduc.com

First published in Great Britain 2002 by
Little Tiger Press
An imprint of Magi Publications

Text Copyright © 2002 by Barbara Bennett
Illustrations Copyright © 2002 by Amanda Hall
Barbara Bennett and Amanda Hall have asserted
their rights to be identified as the author and
illustrator of this work.

All rights reserved

Library of Congress No. 2001098220
International Standard Book No. 0-7641-5533-4

Printed in Belgium
9 8 7 6 5 4 3 2 1

Lion's Precious Gift

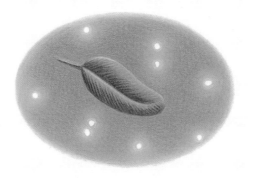

Barbara Bennett
illustrated by Amanda Hall

BARRON'S

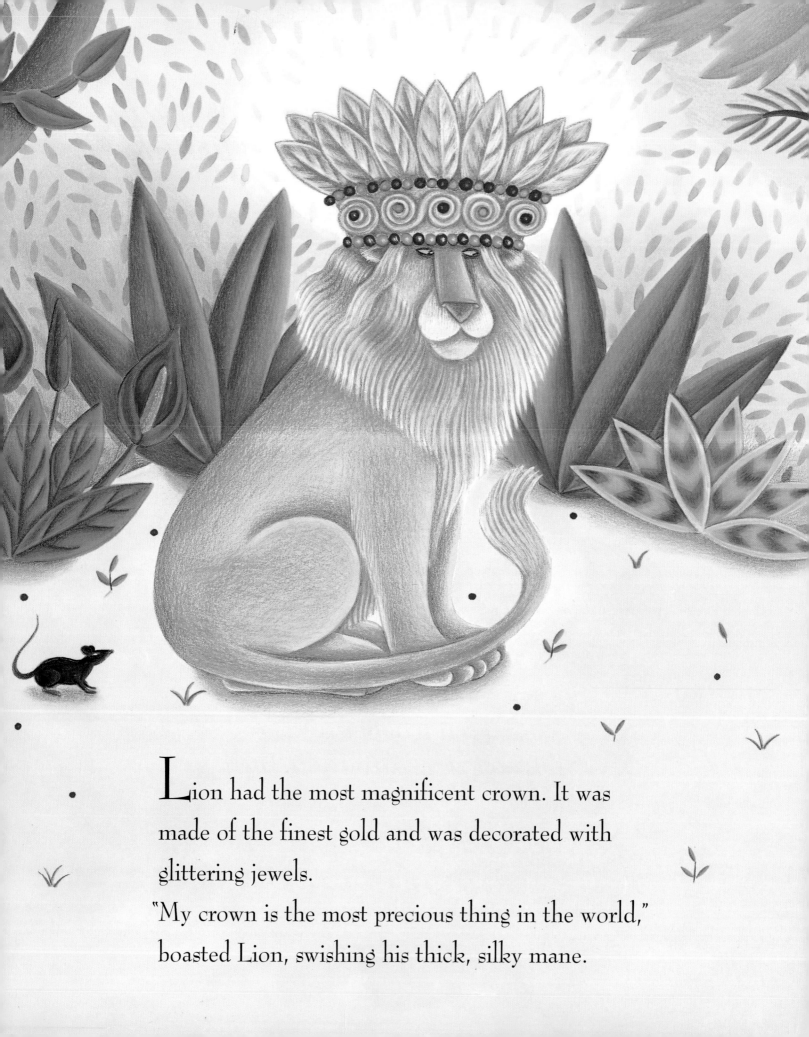

Lion had the most magnificent crown. It was made of the finest gold and was decorated with glittering jewels.

"My crown is the most precious thing in the world," boasted Lion, swishing his thick, silky mane.

"But the world is full of many other magnificent things,"
said Lioness. "If someone brought you an even more
precious gift would you swap it for your crown?"
"Very well then," Lion replied. "Whoever brings me
such a gift shall receive my crown as a prize."

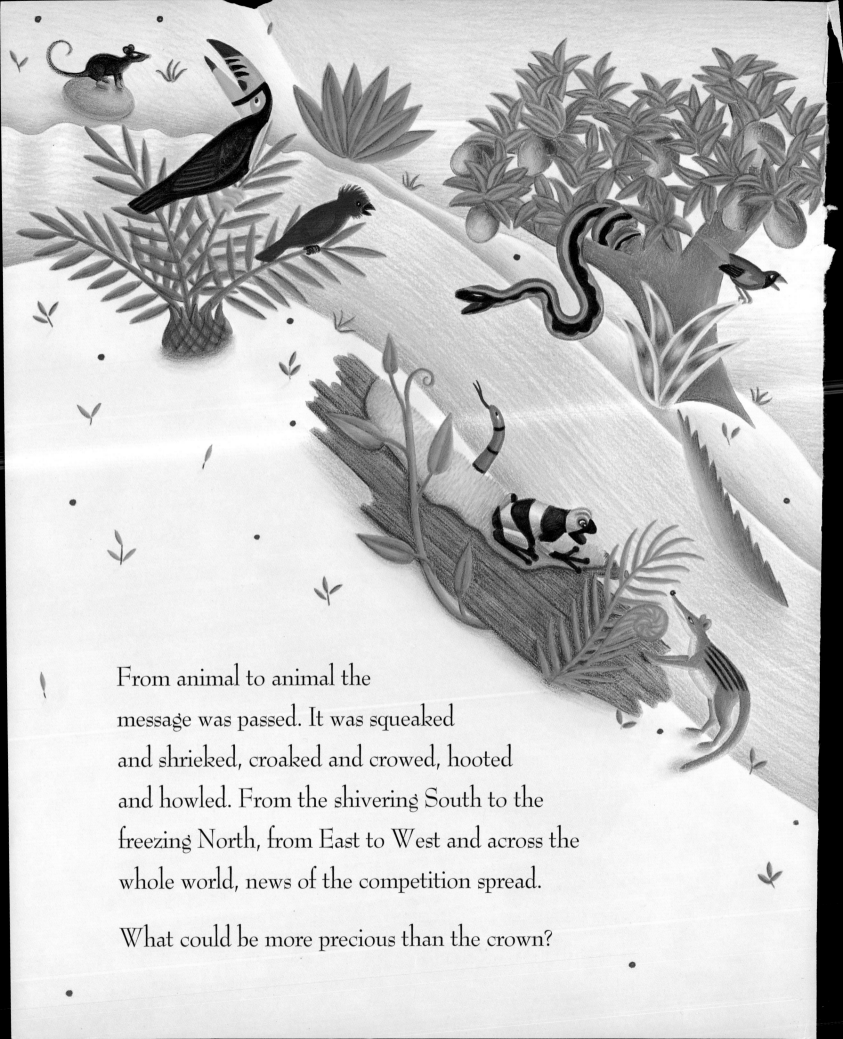

From animal to animal the
message was passed. It was squeaked
and shrieked, croaked and crowed, hooted
and howled. From the shivering South to the
freezing North, from East to West and across the
whole world, news of the competition spread.

What could be more precious than the crown?

That night, every animal dreamed its
own dream. Polar Bear dreamed of huge,
snowy mountains and vast frozen icicles.

Tiger dreamed of splendid colored
stripes of red and yellow, green and blue.

Eagle dreamed of spreading his wings
and flying into the moonlight, to the
edge of the sky and back.

Early next morning, Polar Bear
lumbered from her icy cave.
She thundered through snowstorms
and blizzards, and strode over igloos
and icebergs, until she reached the
top of the world.

With a deafening CRACK she
snapped off the tip of the North Pole,
and headed back south toward
the jungle.

3 1833 04242 7095

That same morning, Tiger threaded
his way stealthily between the flowers
and the ferns, under the bushes and
out on to the grassland.

There, glistening through the bright sun, Tiger saw
a beautiful rainbow arching down to the ground.
With a gigantic POUNCE he snatched the dazzling
stripes from the sky and bounded back to the jungle.

Eagle rested until the night
clouds covered the sky. In the darkness,
he stretched his vast wings and took
off from his nest. Up, up, and away he flew,
towering high above the treetops.

Higher and higher the eagle soared,
above the clouds and between the
twinkling stars, until finally he landed
on the moon. With a quick PECK of his
sharp beak, he broke off a piece of
the moon and glided back home.

Polar Bear, Tiger, and Eagle were the last to arrive
in Lion's clearing. Many other animals had been
and gone, disappointed, for nothing had been found
to equal Lion's magnificent crown.
"In this bag," said Polar Bear, stepping forward,
"I have the most precious gift! It is the freezing North,
to keep you cool in the heat of the day."

She tipped open the bag, but out spilled two
tiny drops of water. Polar Bear stared in disbelief.
The freezing North was gone!
"Foolish bear," sighed Lion. "Don't you know that
ice melts in hot places? Your gift is quite useless."

Next, Tiger stepped forward.

"My gift is the most precious," he boasted.

"In this box I have brought you the stripes of the rainbow. How wonderful you will look, wearing them."

He opened the box, but it was completely empty.
Lion tossed his magnificent mane.
"You are even more foolish than Bear," he said.
"Don't you know that a rainbow will fade and
disappear without the sun and the rain?"

Finally, it was Eagle's turn. He spread his wings and proudly presented his gift at Lion's feet. "I give you the light of the moon in exchange for the crown," he screeched. "That is the most precious gift!"

Lion gave an enormous roar.
"You are the most foolish creature of all.
Don't you know the moon can only shine
in the evening sky? Here in the jungle it is
nothing but a piece of rock."

Polar Bear, Tiger, and Eagle crept away,
shamefaced and disappointed.
As Lion sat in his glittering, sparkling
crown, he felt himself very wise. "Lioness
was quite wrong," he thought. "There is
nothing so precious as my crown. I will
go and tell her so."

Lion padded off across the clearing and through
the undergrowth. "Where is Lioness?" he wondered.
Before long, from behind the bushes, he heard
her deep-throated purr. Lion parted the bushes.

There, in the soft green grass, lay Lioness, and curled
up beside her was their tiny lion cub!
"Look," she purred proudly. "Our baby has been born!"

No jeweled crown could make Lion as proud and happy
as he felt at that moment. As he gently licked and nuzzled
his newborn cub, he laid the crown at Lioness's feet.
"Now I understand," he said. "For what you have given me
is truly the most precious gift of all!"